MW01061851

Danger Canyon

by Margo Sorenson

To Jim, Jane, and Jill, who believed in the dream.
To my parents, who always encouraged dreaming.
To Jody, my editor, who made the dream a reality.

M. S.

Cover Illustration: Donna Rae Nelson
Inside Illustration: Michael A. Aspengren

© 1996 Perfection Learning®
First ebook edition 2012
www.perfectionlearning.com

20 21 22 23 24 25 QG 17 16 15 14 13 12

48525

PB ISBN: 978-0-7891-0227-0
RLB ISBN: 978-0-7807-5506-2
eISBN: 978-1-6138-4934-7

Printed in the United States of America

400583701

Contents

SAN
MIGUEL
CREEK

1
Not Again

"Wasn't Lawrence in trouble again at school this week?" Calvin's mother asked.

How does she know? Calvin wondered. Why was she always checking up on him and his friends? So what if some of his friends got into trouble? Calvin never did.

"Oh, Mom, that was nothing," Calvin lied. "He just had to stay after school. The math teacher hates him—for no reason. It was no big deal."

Calvin leaned forward on the sofa. He quickly flipped channels on the TV. He turned up the volume. Mom has to get off this subject, he thought.

Football players filled the screen. The stadium crowd yelled in the background.

"And it's a 13-yard rush for Donnie Warwick. First and goal for the Vikings!" the announcer shouted.

"Calvin, I'm talking to you," his mother said. She put her hands on her hips.

How could he get her to leave him alone? He hadn't done anything, had he?

"Mom! The Vikings are playing!" Calvin frowned.

"Calvin!" Mom stepped between Calvin and the T.V. She turned down the volume. The she turned to face Calvin.

Calvin sighed. He slumped back against the cushions.

"Tell me about Lawrence. I need to know what's going on with your friends."

"Aw, Mom, I told you it's no big deal. Anyway, I have other friends, you know. Like Rob."

Calvin's mother shook her head. But she was smiling. "Crazy Rob! You'll be lucky if he doesn't get you into a real mess some day!"

"Aw, Mom, come on!" Calvin grinned back. "Rob just likes to have a good time."

"You watch him, though," his mother warned. "He likes to rush off without thinking."

That's true, Calvin admitted to himself. But that made Rob fun to be around. Rob was a good guy. He never did anything bad—just stupid. Calvin hid a smile. It was fun to have a friend like Rob. Calvin always thought things out. He planned things carefully. Rob sure didn't.

Besides, why was his mom always so worried about his friends? None of his friends would end up in real trouble—like with the cops. His mom didn't even know what she was talking about. His friends get into real trouble? No way!

"You know Rob's okay," Calvin said. "He's almost like a brother to me."

"You've got plenty of brothers already," his mother said. "Uh-oh! The potatoes!" She rushed back into the kitchen.

Sure, he had plenty of brothers—and sisters too. But his four brothers and two sisters were all a lot older. Most of them were married and had kids.

His mother returned from the kitchen. "We almost lost the potatoes," she said, brushing off her apron. "Calvin, I'm talking to you. Look at me, please."

Calvin sighed and looked at his mom.

"Honestly, when your father is away on a long haul, I think you send me your evil twin."

"Aw, Mom," he complained. "What did I do? Nothin'!"

His mother sighed. "Listen, Calvin, we're going to

7

Melveen's this weekend," she said. "I want to help your sister with the new baby."

"Again? But Mom," Calvin began.

"There's no reason for us to stay in the city this weekend," his mother interrupted. "Your father is a thousand miles away from here, and he won't be home until next week."

She sighed. "Besides, the crime makes me nervous these days. I like to get away from the city whenever we can."

"But Mom, I gotta see my friends," Calvin said. "I go to school all week. I have to do homework after school. Or I have football practice. There's never any time to do stuff with my friends." He slumped down into the cushions.

His mother pursed her lips. "Maybe that's just as well," she said.

"What do you mean?" Calvin asked. He sat up straighter. Did his mom think he shouldn't hang out with his buddies? "Hey, I'm responsible. And my friends are too—pretty much. Why can't I just stay home by myself?"

Mom chuckled. "Not likely," she said. "That's out. Well, we're going. You'll have fun," she said. "You'll see."

"Sure, baby-sitting CeeCee while you and Melveen talk for hours," Calvin muttered.

"How about a hike?" his mother said. "You've gone

on some nice ones before. They have all those trails practically right behind their house in that little city park."

"Those are baby hikes," Calvin said. He made a face. "I even saw a Brownie troop there last weekend."

Suddenly, a new thought popped into his head. "Hey, maybe a hike's not such a bad idea after all!" Calvin exclaimed. "I could go up to the big park—the national park. I can hike a long way there. Harold has been telling me to do that. He says they've got some great trails."

His mother looked worried. "I don't know," she said. "I'd feel better if you stayed in the city park. There are things about hiking that city boys don't know."

Calvin sunk back down into the sofa.

"It can be dangerous," Mom said. "I think they've had some problems up there with mountain lions too. I just saw on a TV program that they're starting to attack people."

"Mountain lions? Oh, Mom, come on!" Calvin protested. "No mountain lion's gonna get me! The park rangers wouldn't let people hike up there if it wasn't safe. You know that!

"Can't I have a little fun? Think about me stuck all weekend with Harold, Melveen, and all those diapers! Besides, you know I'm responsible," Calvin finished.

His mother smiled at him. "Well, there is the park ranger station right there." She paused. "I guess it would probably be okay. But you need to take a friend—the right kind of friend. I don't want you hiking alone." She frowned. "You never know what might happen on a hike. It could be dangerous."

"I know that, Mom," Calvin sighed. "I've read a lot about hiking and stuff like that. I'll be careful." He enjoyed books about outdoor survival. He really liked Gary Paulsen's books.

His mother smiled. "All right. You can go."

"Yeah!" he said. Suddenly, the weekend was looking better. If he couldn't stay home with his friends, at least he could take a friend with him.

"Why don't you ask Phillip?" his mother continued. "He's a nice boy."

"Come on, Mom! Phillip's weird," Calvin said. "I want to have a good time. I don't want to feel like I'm in the library. All Phillip likes to do is study."

"Well, there's nothing wrong with that," his mother said. She untied her apron. "Dinner's ready."

"I'll ask Rob," Calvin said. "He's gone hiking before."

Rob would be fun. He'd be a great friend for an adventure. He would try anything.

****

After dinner, Calvin washed the dishes. "I'm gonna call Rob, Mom," he said as he finished. He wiped the last plate and put it away.

"Don't make it too long," his mother said. "It's just about time for your father to call. I don't want the phone busy."

Calvin reached for the phone. He quickly punched in Rob's number.

"Hello?" Rob's voice came through the phone.

"Rob? Calvin. Hey man, what are you doing this weekend?"

"Oh, nothin' much. Thought I'd practice for the NCAA Final Four," Rob joked. He played basketball. He was the school's top scorer.

"How about coming with me to my sister's?"

"What?" Rob asked. "You gotta be kidding."

"No! Just wait. Hear me out. You know how she and her husband got this new house in San Miguel?"

"I know," Rob said. "You complain every time you have to go there."

"Yeah, but listen." Calvin's words tumbled out. "They live in this new subdivision. It's way out of town. But it's right next to a national park. My mom says I can go on a long hike. But I need to take a friend. How 'bout it? It'll be great!"

"Hey!" Rob said. He began to sound excited. "Okay! Let me ask my mom."

Clunk! Rob dropped the phone.

"Ouch!" Calvin said. He rubbed his ear. Rob always did that. Calvin strained to listen. He could hear Rob's mother's voice. She sounded mad. Then he heard Rob. Then Rob's mom said something again.

Rob came back on the phone. "She says it's okay. She says it can be dangerous. Especially for us 'city boys.' " Rob sounded disgusted. "Like we're babies or something! But she finally said all right. 'After all, Calvin is such a responsible boy,' she said!" Rob laughed. "Still foolin' them, aren't you?" he joked.

"Great!" Calvin said happily. "We'll pick you up after school tomorrow."

They said good-bye and hung up. Great is right, Calvin thought. He smiled. The weekend was looking up. He and Rob would have fun on a long hike.

He couldn't understand why his mom was concerned. How could hiking be dangerous? It's just walking in the woods!

2

They've Escaped!

His mother turned off the car engine. The sun was setting. The lights were already on in Melveen and Harold's little house. It looked just like the others on the entire street, Calvin thought. No, it looked like all the others in the entire subdivision. The subdivision was way out of town. It was right next to the mountains. But that made it kind of cool.

At least Melveen and Harold could buy a house, he admitted. They were excited, even though it was small. It was their very own.

Calvin looked at the mountains looming up in the twilight. Somehow in the darkness, they almost looked scary. He felt a little shiver run down his spine.

"There's Grandma!" Melveen's voice broke into Calvin's thoughts. He looked through the window to see Melveen holding his niece, CeeCee. She was bouncing CeeCee up and down in her arms. CeeCee's chubby cheeks were jiggling.

"Gammah!" CeeCee cried. She held out a sticky hand to Calvin's mom.

"Look, Jacob, there's Grandma!" Harold walked up holding a tiny blue bundle in his big arms.

Hugs and greetings over, they all trooped into the house. Calvin lugged in his suitcase and sleeping bag. Rob carried his duffel bag and sleeping bag. They dropped everything down in the front room.

Calvin's mom took the baby into the kitchen. Calvin could hear his mom cooing, "That's Grandma's little sweetie. Yes it is!" Why was it that people always talked to babies in high little voices? he wondered.

Rob and Calvin walked to the big picture window. "Hey, how would you two city boys like to sleep outside?" Harold asked. "It's not that cold out at night yet." He sat down on the couch. "That way, there'll be more room in here. And it'll be more of an adventure for you indoor kids." He grinned.

Melveen looked sharply at him. "Harold," she said. "I told you that wasn't a good idea."

Calvin and Rob looked at each other. What's going on? Calvin wondered.

"Come on, honey," Harold said. He shook his head. "These guys are big boys. Why don't you go on in and talk to your mother?" He smiled.

Melveen frowned. "All right, I'll leave it up to your best judgment. But you know how I feel about that mountain lion stuff. The Johnsons are sure a mountain lion got their cat just last week. And we don't let CeeCee play outside alone," Melveen reminded him. She picked up a baby rattle and walked into the kitchen.

"What's she talking about?" Calvin asked. If there was something going on about mountain lions, he wanted to know.

"Mountain lions?" Rob said excitedly.

"No mountain lion is going to come down and attack you!" Harold grinned at them. "We're a ways from the national park. Besides, the rangers are pretty sure they already shot the only mountain lion around."

"So, how come mountain lions were around the houses? Don't they just stay in the forest?" Calvin asked.

"It's because this subdivision is so close to the mountains. The park rangers think that the new houses crowded them out. So it's possible that the lions still come back here. They think it's still their territory."

"Have you seen one?" Rob asked excitedly.

"No," Harold said. He grinned. "But Melveen's friend Sue from a few blocks away thought she saw one through the brush behind her house. And then there's the Johnsons' cat. She's missing, and Melveen is sure a mountain lion got her."

Harold shook his head. "You see, boys? It's just hearsay."

"The little girl who was attacked up in the national park wasn't hearsay!" Melveen interrupted. She had walked back into the room for the baby's bottle. She frowned at Harold.

"Someone got attacked?" Calvin asked. This did sound a little scary. Maybe they shouldn't go on a long hike in the national park after all.

"She was picking flowers by herself off the trail. A mountain lion attacked her. Luckily, her father came up. He hit the lion with a baseball bat. She had to have surgery on her face." Melveen shuddered. "That's why we are so careful with CeeCee."

"Could we get attacked too?" Calvin wondered aloud.

"Nah," Harold said with a wide grin. "The rangers already tracked the lion and shot it. They'd close the park if they thought it was dangerous.

"Besides," Harold continued, "the girl was off the trail. You're never supposed to get off a trail. And she was only three years old. She was really small. You turkeys are too big and ugly for a mountain lion to attack." He grinned at them.

"Cool!" Rob said, grinning. "I'd like to see one! How

big are they?"

"Now, Harold, aren't you forgetting about that woman jogger who was killed by a mountain lion?" Melveen asked.

"Melveen! What's wrong with your geography? That was way up north. Plus, it wasn't in a park. She was jogging in the woods. These guys will be fine. Let 'em sleep outside."

"I'll sleep with my flashlight," Rob said. "If a mountain lion wakes me up, I'll shine it in his eyes!" Rob's eyes gleamed with mischief. "He'll freeze! Then I'll whack him on the head with the flashlight! A mountain-lion rug would look cool in my room!"

Calvin laughed. Melveen and Harold began to laugh too. "You are crazy, Rob!" Calvin said.

"You can't go around being afraid of everything," Rob said. "We'll be fine sleeping outside. I'll watch for mountain lions!"

"Melveen! Come and see this!" Calvin's mother called from the kitchen.

Melveen walked back into the kitchen.

Harold turned up the TV.

"It's USC on UCLA's 40-yard line," the announcer said. "Time out, UCLA."

"All right!" Rob said.

"No way! UCLA's the team, man!" Calvin joked.

Commercials blared from the TV.

We interrupt this program for a special news
bulletin from your local station. Two juvenile
prisoners from the Carlson Forestry Detention
Camp near the San Miguel National Forest
escaped this afternoon. They may be armed.
They are considered dangerous. Residents in the
area should be on the lookout. Keep your doors
locked.

"San Miguel! That's right up here in the mountains, isn't it?" Calvin asked. He didn't like the sound of escaped prisoners!

"We don't have anything to worry about. That forestry camp is ten miles away. The escapees wouldn't come to a little development like this. They'll want to get to the city as quickly as possible. And besides, the cops will find them pretty fast. Those city boys don't do too well in the forest," Harold said.

Calvin felt his stomach turn a flip. Escapees? From the detention camp? Guys who had blown other guys away were sent to those camps. He had even seen some of the guys from that camp once. They had been on a work detail in the city park.

He had been on one of his short hikes. He had come around a bend and there they were—ten tough-looking guys dressed in orange jumpsuits. They were picking up trash from the side of the trail. They weren't much older than he was. Two guards stood near them, watching. A couple of the prisoners stopped working. They turned to stare at him. Calvin shivered, remembering. He could still remember how mean they looked.

Now, two of them had escaped. What had the two escapees done to get themselves sent to camp? Had they stolen cars? Had they shot someone? Sure, he knew some guys who got into big trouble at school. But none of his friends got into any real trouble with cops.

"This is great!" Rob said. "The mountain lion can take care of the guys from the camp!" He grinned widely.

Harold spoke up. "Those guys won't have time to tangle with a mountain lion. They won't last long in the mountains," he said again. "These mountains are tougher than they look. Especially for street boys."

Whew, Calvin thought. Lucky his mother wasn't in the room to hear this!

"This is really gonna be great tomorrow!" Rob said excitedly. "Maybe we could catch those guys! Then we could be on the evening news! We could get medals!"

Calvin thought about Rob's comments. Yeah, it would be great to be heroes. But messing with criminals didn't seem like a good idea. Those guys would be pretty desperate. They'd have to be desperate to want to escape. They probably wouldn't stop at anything, Calvin thought. He flinched.

Why doesn't Rob ever seem to be afraid? wondered Calvin. He decided he'd try to be more like Rob. Just don't worry about it till it happens.

"So, we'll sleep outside tonight. We'll get used to the

outdoors. And maybe we'll even bag us a mountain lion—or an escaped convict!" Rob went on. He grinned at Calvin.

Calvin smiled back, weakly.

Mountain lions? Escaped convicts? Maybe this hike tomorrow wasn't such a great idea after all.

3

This Is Going to Be Great!

It was early morning. Calvin and Rob were standing in Melveen's small kitchen. They had been making their lunches. Jars of peanut butter and jelly were all over the counter.

Plop! Rob dropped his lunch and three sodas into Calvin's backpack.

"Hey!" Calvin said. "Don't squish my sandwich, you weasel!" He shifted the backpack on his shoulders. "What do you have in there, anyway? Enough food for the whole Marine base?" He grinned at Rob.

"Okay, okay! I told you I'd carry it sometimes too!" Rob said. "You're such a wimp!" he joked.

"Wimps don't hike," Calvin said. How true that had become!

Calvin remembered what a hard time he'd had getting to sleep last night. He had tossed and turned in his sleeping bag. First, he thought he heard a police helicopter in the distance. That sent chills down his spine. He knew they must be looking for the escaped prisoners. It was like being back home in the city. He waited and watched for the huge "midnight sun" searchlight. But no helicopter ever appeared.

Then he thought he heard strange noises behind the fence. It sounded like rustling. He had opened his eyes wide. He strained to see into the darkness. If only he could see! Was it a mountain lion? Was it prowling around? Was it waiting for them to fall asleep? Or was it the guys who escaped from the camp? Would they jump them in the dark?

You dummy, he had scolded himself. Hadn't Harold said the rangers had shot the mountain lion? Hadn't Harold said the escapees wouldn't come this way? Shape up, Calvin told himself. How could he face defensive linemen on the football field if he couldn't sleep outside in a housing development?

He had finally fallen asleep. The last time he looked at the lighted dial of his watch, it had been one in the morning. Not much sleep before a day of hiking. Well, too bad. He'd just have to be tough.

Calvin sighed. Too much had come up. He wasn't sure he still wanted to hike. But he couldn't let Rob know. Rob would never let him forget it.

"Now remember," Harold said, looking up from his breakfast. "City boys aren't used to these mountains. This isn't like playing a video game down at the arcade. Don't go thinking you're macho. Stay on the marked trail." He put a bit of egg in his mouth. "I don't feel like giving up my Saturday to look for a couple of lost lame-brains!" He grinned. "I gotta watch the football game."

"Harold!" Melveen scolded.

"Now, Mel, these guys know I'm just giving them a hard time," Harold said, smiling.

Calvin's mother looked worried. "Maybe you should stay in the city park. Maybe you should just hike on one of the shorter trails."

"Mom, you promised. We'll be okay," Calvin whined. "Don't make us hike with all the Brownie troops," he added.

"Don't worry, Mrs. Greene," Rob said. "I've gone hiking before. And Calvin's a smart dude. We'll be fine."

"You know I'm responsible," Calvin chimed in. "Aren't you always saying how you want me to be independent?"

"You two should take the Canyon Trail," Melveen told them. She turned to her mother. "It's not hard, Mom.

It's well-marked," she continued.

Calvin gave Melveen a grateful look. Maybe big sisters weren't that bad after all. At least Melveen and Harold hadn't said anything to his mom about the mountain lions—yet. That would really scare her.

"Be sure to stop at the ranger station. Let them know you'll be hiking today. And get a trail map," cautioned Melveen. "Do you have everything you need?"

"Yeah, I think so," Calvin said.

"Don't worry," Rob said. "You know Calvin. He thinks of everything. He's got a flashlight, some matches, extra water, and our lunches in the backpack."

Harold watched and waited as Melveen and her mom took CeeCee into the other room. Then he looked at the boys and grinned slyly.

"Did you remember handcuffs for the escapees?" Harold joked. He chuckled. "You're gonna catch 'em, aren't you?"

Calvin's stomach did a little flip. Not funny, he thought.

Harold swabbed up some egg with a piece of toast. "Seriously, you might see some homeless people up there. They go up to live in the woods. But they shouldn't bother you. They don't want to be found."

Calvin's mother walked back into the kitchen. She frowned at Harold's last words. "You two be extra careful out there. Be sure and give yourself enough time. You need to be off the mountain by sundown. You can't hike in the dark."

"Oh, Mom, come on," Calvin complained. "Melveen says this is an easy day's hike. We're not hiking to the moon!"

The two boys shut the door behind them. They began walking down the quiet streets. A few people were already out mowing their lawns.

"I'm glad we're getting an early start," Calvin said. "That way, we'll have plenty of time."

"No sweat," Rob answered. They looked up at the huge mountains ahead.

"Look!" Calvin said. He pointed. "You can see the firebreak road from here. That's how we get to the ranger station."

Calvin shaded his eyes against the early morning sun. The road cut a slash across the green, pine-covered slopes. Then it wound up and up to a small, flat plateau. Calvin could just barely make out a few buildings on the plateau. Those must be the rangers' quarters. The park rangers lived and worked on the mountain.

Beyond the rangers' buildings stood the tree-covered slopes of the San Miguelito Mountains. Calvin felt his heart race a little in excitement. This would be an adventure all right.

"What would it be like living in the middle of a forest?" Calvin wondered aloud. He was so used to living in a city apartment. He couldn't imagine hearing pine trees blowing in the wind at night.

"Pretty quiet," Rob answered. "No traffic and noisy mufflers," he said with a grin.

The boys began walking uphill. They reached the edge of the housing development. The road led onto a bridge over a big stream. They passed a sign that read

Rob stopped and stared over the bridge railing. The water moved swiftly below. "Awesome!" he said. "We should go swimming in this some time."

"It's going pretty fast for a swim," Calvin answered. "It's cold too. It drains all the snow from way up in the mountains."

Just past the bridge was a sign that read

They walked through the park on the gravel road. Their tennis shoes crunched on the stones. Pine trees rustled above them. The park was quiet. No one else was there this early.

Finally, they saw a big, brown, wooden sign that read

Underneath it hung a smaller sign.

Posted next to that was another sign. Calvin read the words across the top.

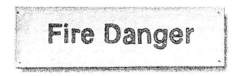

Underneath, someone had hung a smaller sign on little hooks. Written in red letters were the words

Great, Calvin thought. So much for the matches. He had felt so smart to remember them. In the books he had read, the characters never had matches when they needed them. Now, they couldn't use them anyway. He hadn't thought about forest fires. He decided hiking wasn't as easy as it sounded.

"This is it," Rob said, turning to grin at Calvin. "This is the beginning of our adventure."

"Here we go," Calvin said. He sounded more confident than he felt.

They trudged up the firebreak road. They passed a young couple. They passed two older people with gray hair. The man had a walking stick.

"If those old geezers can do this, we can too," Rob assured Calvin. They laughed.

In half an hour, they reached the trim green and white buildings of the ranger station. Pine needles crunched on the path beneath their tennis shoes. Calvin took a deep breath. The pine trees smelled fresh and clean. How different this was from the car exhaust fumes in the city! Calvin stopped on the path and stared at the ranger station.

"Hey, it looks closed," Calvin said. He tried the door. It was locked. He looked around. "I don't see anyone," he said, a little worried. The building next to the office looked like it might be the rangers' house. It looked like it was locked up tightly. The window shades were down.

"Look, there's a sign," Rob said. He pointed to the window of the office. The boys both read it.

Hours:

6 AM to 6 PM
Monday – Friday
9 AM to 6 PM
Saturday and Sunday

"Well, it's Saturday all right. What time is it?" he asked Calvin.

Calvin looked at his watch. "It's only 8:15," he answered, frowning. "How are we going to get a trail map?"

"Aw, we don't need a trail map. I'm sure they'll have markers along the way," Rob said importantly. "When I went hiking with my church group last summer in Yosemite, that's what we used."

Calvin frowned. "I don't really want to do this without a map," he said.

"You're always too careful," Rob said. "Even your sister said the trail was well-marked."

"Yeah," Calvin said slowly. "But even so, we should let them know we're up here hiking. Like my sister said. So, let's just wait till they open."

"Come on, man. Only wimps and little old ladies register with the park ranger," Rob said impatiently. He turned around and began walking toward a wooden sign. "Let's get going. I'm not waiting any 45 minutes until the park ranger comes."

Rob stopped in front of the sign. "Besides," he said over his shoulder to Calvin, "I bet we won't have time to do the whole hike if we wait."

He's got a point, Calvin decided. "Okay," he said a little unwillingly. "I guess it's probably okay." He began walking back over to the path where Rob stood under the pines.

"Look!" Rob pointed to the sign. "Look at this."

"It shows the whole trail going this way. It says to follow the green painted signs! I told you so," he said proudly. He grinned at Calvin. "We don't have a thing to worry about. This is going to be great!"

Calvin felt a little better. Maybe Rob was right. They probably could follow the trail without a map.

But two little nagging thoughts pushed their way into his head—mountain lions and escaped prisoners. In that case, map or no map, well-marked or not, it wouldn't matter.

4

Someone Has Been Here!

"Let's go!" Rob said. He walked briskly down the path.

"Hold on," Calvin said. He walked over to the water fountain. He drank deeply. He felt worn out already. It was quite a hike just up the firebreak road. He must be extra tired because of last night.

"Hurry up!" Rob said. He kept walking but went more slowly. "Hey! Look at this! Cool!"

"What is it?" Calvin asked. He hurried to catch up with Rob.

Rob pointed ahead of him. "That's the same stream that we saw down below. The sign even says so—San Miguel Creek! It must run all the way down through the canyon! Cool!" he repeated.

The creek rushed between rocky banks. The water looked clean and clear. It pulsed around boulders. White, frothy foam bubbled up and splashed. Calvin felt the spray. It cooled him off.

"The trail leads right beside the stream," Rob said. "Great! I wish we had brought fishing poles!"

"We'd need a license to fish," Calvin said.

"Not if no one saw us!" Rob said, grinning. "How about that? We could catch our own fish. Then we could cook them over a campfire!"

Calvin sighed. "Yeah, that would be fun. But that's all illegal."

"What do you mean?" Rob asked.

"We'd need a license for the fish. Even if we had one, we couldn't start a fire. Didn't you see the sign at the trail head? No open fires?" Calvin asked. Rob never pays attention to anything, he thought.

"Nope. Guess I didn't," Rob admitted. "It's a good thing you're around to make sure we follow all the rules, Mr. Responsible!" he teased Calvin. "Oh well, maybe another time. Anyway, let's go!"

Rob began making his way down the trail. He hopped over rocks and crunched fallen pine cones. Calvin hurried to catch up. Together, they hiked down the trail. The backpack thumped against Calvin's back. It was beginning to feel heavy.

Next to them, the creek rushed past tree roots and bubbled over rocks. The breeze was rustling the pines. The air smelled fresh and woodsy. All around them was quiet, except for the sound of the rushing water.

This is great, Calvin thought. No mountain lions, either. He smiled to himself. Now he felt sure Harold was right. The rangers must have killed the mountain lion that had attacked the girl. It was too peaceful up here for any mountain lion to be prowling around.

Rob had already turned the bend in the trail.

"Hey!" he yelled. "Look at these!"

Calvin came around the bend. He saw a clearing next to the creek. Three cabins stood clustered together. One looked like a real log cabin. One was painted red. The third, at the edge of the clearing, was white.

"Cool!" Rob exclaimed. "I wonder who lives here?"

They stopped in front of the log cabin. There were flowerpots by the front door. The flowers were blooming bright pink. But pine cones and pine needles lay on the porch. The window shades were pulled down.

"No one has been here for a while," Rob said. He walked around the side of the porch.

Calvin felt a little funny. How could Rob be so sure no one had been there? The cabins were easy to get to. And they were right on the trail. They would make a great place to hide. Say, for someone (or two someones) who didn't want to be found. Calvin frowned. He had to get that idea out of his head.

"I bet this is someone's vacation cabin," Calvin said. He couldn't imagine what it would be like to own two houses. His family didn't own even one house.

Rob was already down at the third cabin.

"This one looks abandoned!" he yelled. "Cool!" Rob climbed up the steps to the porch. The front door sagged in. There was no doorknob. Before Calvin knew it, Rob was leaning on the front door. He shoved it, hard.

"Unnh!" he grunted.

"Hey! What do you think you're doing?" Calvin hollered.

Pop! Just then, the door gave way. Rob almost fell in. He held onto the door frame.

"Come on in," Rob said. Calvin stopped at the edge of the porch. "Come on, you wimp!"

"All right, I'm coming," Calvin muttered. He carefully walked across the porch and peered inside. He didn't like this at all. But Rob was already in the front room.

"Check this out!" Rob called.

Calvin walked in. Rob was pointing up above the fireplace. Calvin's eyes followed his finger.

"Awesome!" Rob said.

"Yeah," Calvin breathed. He saw the head of a huge black bear snarling at him from above the fireplace. Its jaws were open, showing yellow, jagged teeth. The person who had stuffed it had even included a red tongue.

Both boys were quiet. They stared at the bear. Its eyes glittered at them.

"How'd you like to meet that puppy on the trail?" Rob finally asked.

"Yeah," Calvin choked. He shivered a little. "Or a mountain lion," he added.

"Mountain lions!" Rob said. "I almost forgot!" He grinned. "This is fun. Let's see what else is here." He turned and walked into a dark hallway.

What if someone is here? Calvin wondered. It was really stupid to go wandering into a strange cabin. They were really trespassing too. He knew it.

"It's dark in here. Where's the flashlight?" Rob asked.

"I'll get it," Calvin said. He walked into the dark hallway. Calvin took off the backpack and unzipped it. He fumbled around for the flashlight. Ah! Got it. It felt cold in his hand. He took it out and handed it to Rob.

"All right," Rob said. He took two steps across the floor. The light from the flashlight danced in front of him.

Wham! "Unnnh!" Rob yelled.

Oh no! Calvin's heart stood still. "Rob? What happened?" he called anxiously.

"Aaah!" Rob yelled. "My ankle!"

Calvin peered through the darkness. The light from the flashlight was gone. Before too long, his eyes got used to the dark. He could see Rob lying on the wooden floor.

"I stepped right through the floor!" Rob moaned.

"The floor's rotten. Don't come this way!"

"Hold on. I'll help you up," Calvin said. "Are you okay?"

"Yeah, I'm fine," Rob said. His teeth sounded as if they were clenched together. "My ankle's just a little twisted. No big deal."

"Where's the flashlight?" Calvin asked.

"Aw, rats! The flashlight. I must have dropped it down the hole. Let's see if we can get it," Rob said.

Calvin walked carefully over to Rob and helped him up. Then they both knelt. They looked down into the empty, black space where the floorboards had rotted away.

"I don't see it, do you?" asked Rob.

"Uh-uh," Calvin said. "You had it turned on, right? We should be able to see the light." He sighed. "Unless it broke when it dropped."

"I'm not going down there to get it, " Rob said. "Who knows what's living down there."

Calvin stared into the inky blackness. "Me either," he said. "Geez," he added. "We really need the flashlight for hiking. All those books say that you never know what might happen."

"Yeah, well all those books are about real, live hikes in the wilderness too," Rob said. "This is just a day hike near your sister's house, remember?" Calvin could see his grin through the darkness.

Had Rob forgotten the guys who escaped from the

detention camp? How about the mountain lions? Calvin bit his tongue. Rob had already called him a wimp today. He didn't need to hear it again.

"Well, that's that," Rob said. He stood up and brushed off some cobwebs. "Let's finish looking around, okay?"

"Well, watch out for the floor," Calvin warned.

"Yeah, okay," Rob said. He limped into the next room. He noticed a damp, spicy smell.

Calvin followed, zipping up the backpack. Something drew Calvin's eyes to the table. He froze.

"Rob," he croaked. "Rob, look!"

Calvin pointed to the table. Sitting there were two open cans of chili. They had spoons in them.

"Aw, those are probably old and all dried up," Rob said. But he didn't look too sure as he stared at the table.

Together, the two boys moved closer to the table. Calvin touched one of the cans—it was warm.

5

What Should We Do?

"Let's get outta here!" Calvin whispered. Rob looked at him strangely. Then he reached out. He touched the can too. Rob jerked his hand back as if it had been burned. He swallowed hard and nodded.

Pretend like nothing's wrong, Calvin told himself. Someone could be watching them right now. Was it some homeless person, like Harold had said? Or was it—Calvin shuddered—the escapees from the detention camp?

He took a deep breath and cleared his throat. "Ah, there's nothin' here. Let's go," he said.

Rob took his cue. "Yeah, you're right," he said. "It's old and wrecked." Together the boys backed away from the table. Then they turned to walk through the dark hallway. Calvin stopped short. Rob ran right into him.

"Hey!" Rob whispered loudly. "What are you doin'?"

Calvin's heart pounded under his shirt. What if someone—or two someones—were waiting for them in the darkness? What could they do? They didn't have anything they could use for a weapon. Rob had lost the flashlight under the house. Well, he'd just have to pretend he was running with a pass for a touchdown right through the defensive backs.

Calvin took a deep breath and started walking very quickly through the darkness. He avoided the hole in the floor. Calvin felt Rob right behind him. When he was out of the dark, Calvin broke into a run. Both boys ran through the front room and past the snarling bear. They raced through the open door and down the porch steps.

Calvin didn't stop when he reached the trail and the creek. He kept going down the trail. The green signs and arrows pointed the way. Rob's footsteps pounded behind him. He could hear Rob favoring his one ankle—thump-THUMP, thump-THUMP.

"Hey, man! What're you doin'? Think you're running for a touchdown or something?" Rob panted.

"We can't stay around here. We gotta figure this out,"

Calvin called back over his shoulder. The backpack thumped heavily against his shoulder blades. He had Rob to thank for all those cans of soda.

Way up ahead, Calvin saw a huge set of boulders. We can climb up on those, he thought. Then they could see all around them. They could decide what they would do next.

Calvin scrambled up the biggest boulder. His knees and tennis shoes scraped on the hard granite. Rob was right behind him.

"Ouch!" Rob said. He looked at his fingers. They were scraped from the rocks. One was bleeding. "Man, we must have run a mile! Aah," he said as he reached down and rubbed his ankle.

Calvin looked carefully around him. First he looked back toward the cabins. No one seemed to be shadowing them through the forest. The trail was clear. Then he scanned the other directions. The pine trees whispered peacefully in the wind. There were no footsteps crunching pine needles or fallen leaves. No shadows darted behind trees. Everything was quiet.

"Whew!" Calvin sighed. He pulled his knees up to his chest and wrapped his arms around them.

"Do you think someone was there, watching us?" Rob asked. He licked the blood from his fingers. He wiped them on his jeans.

"I don't know," Calvin admitted. "Should we go back to the ranger station and tell them?" he asked slowly.

Rob frowned. "Nah," he said. "It's probably just some poor, homeless person. They need all the breaks they can get. My sister-in-law was talking about a homeless person she knows," he said. "Lost her job. She couldn't pay the rent. She had a sick kid too. So first she was living in her car. Now she's in a homeless shelter," he said, shaking his head.

"But what if it's the guys who escaped from the forestry detention camp? The prisoners?" Calvin asked. His heart beat a little faster even as he spoke.

Rob snorted. "Listen, do you think they'd let us get away?"

"Why wouldn't they?" Calvin asked.

"Lots of reasons. They would have seen the backpack. We have stuff they need. Besides, we could tell the police they were there." Rob's face drained of color. "That's why they'd have to kill us."

Calvin shuddered. "Yeah," he agreed slowly. "I guess you're right. I never thought of it like that."

"You gotta think like a criminal, man," Rob joked. He smiled weakly.

Calvin returned his smile. But he could feel sweat breaking out on his forehead.

"Besides," Rob went on, "how many escapees from a detention camp would carry cans of chili when they ran?" He snickered. "Not too many."

"True," Calvin said. He scratched a twig back and forth on the granite. It rasped against the stone. He frowned. "But the chili could have been in the cabin, and they found it."

Rob sighed. "Did you see how dusty that cabin was? It's probably been years since anyone has lived there. I'm sure there wasn't anything left to eat. Anyway, like I said, they would have killed us." Rob put his hands around his throat in a choking motion. "Aaaaargh!" he choked, sticking out his tongue.

Calvin laughed in spite of himself. "All right," he said, grinning. "You win. It was probably some homeless people. So, I guess we don't go back and tell the rangers, right?"

"Right," Rob said. "And we finish our hike."

Calvin looked at his watch. "Okay," he said, "we've been gone for almost two hours. Let's keep going for a couple more hours before we turn around. We may not finish the hike all the way to the end of the trail. But at least we'll be off the mountain by dark."

"Sounds good to me," Rob agreed.

Calvin relaxed. Up here, on top of the boulders, they could see a long way. Below them, the mountain dropped off steeply. The trail continued beside the creek. They could hear the creek rushing over rocks. Straight over the tops of the pine trees, they could see the town of San Miguel in the valley below.

"This is cool," Rob said. "How about lunch? I'm starving."

"It's only ten o'clock," Calvin said. "If we eat now,

we won't have anything left at lunchtime."

"You sound like my mother," Rob complained. "First you lead me on a million-yard touchdown run. So I work up an appetite. Then you tell me I can't eat because I'll spoil my lunch?"

"Okay," Calvin agreed. "Let's eat. But let's save some, just in case."

"Just in case what?" Rob asked.

"You never know," Calvin said. "In those adventure books..."

"Real life isn't like a book, Calvin," Rob said. "Get off it, will you?" He grinned to take the edge off his remark. "Now," he said, grabbing for the backpack, "what's in here?"

"Not so fast," Calvin said. He snatched the backpack away quickly. "Ha! Gotcha," he said, smiling. "Now *I'll* decide what we eat."

"Oh yeah?" Rob yelled. He made a grab for Calvin's shirt, but Calvin was too fast for him. Rob fell back onto the boulder. Calvin laughed.

"Geez!" Rob said loudly. "I'm gonna be a mass of bruises after this hike."

"Whatsa matter? Can't take the rough-tough outdoors?" Calvin teased.

Rob looked disgusted. "Give me my sandwich, will you?" He stared at Calvin. Calvin just grinned.

"All right—please!" Rob sighed.

Calvin handed him his sandwich and a soda. The

Suddenly, a streak of yellow flashed below. It raced back into the forest.

"Holy cow!" Calvin yelled. He sat up. "It was a mountain lion! I saw it! I saw it!"

Rob scrambled over. He looked in the direction Calvin was looking.

"Are you sure?" Rob asked. "I don't see anything." He peered into the light and shadows of the forest.

Calvin strained his eyes. It was hard to tell what was a shadow of a tree and what might be something else. "I know it!" he cried. "It was yellow! And could it move! It was fast!"

Rob looked doubtful. "Are you sure it wasn't a big chipmunk?" he asked. "A squirrel? A deer? Or maybe someone's dog? Mountain lions don't like to get close to people, do they?"

"I swear it looked like one," Calvin said. But then he stopped. He hadn't actually gotten a good look at it. All he had seen was a yellow flash. "Maybe you're right," Calvin admitted. "I am kinda jumpy today."

He kept looking in the direction where he had seen the flash disappear. He narrowed his eyes. Did he see something again? No, it was just the shifting pattern of the branches blowing. He sighed.

"You gotta calm down," Rob said. "Or this hike is gonna be a disaster." He grinned.

"Okay." Calvin finished his sandwich and drank his soda. He stuffed two cookies in his mouth. "Let's go," he said.

"All right," Rob said.

They carefully climbed down the face of the boulder. Calvin jumped onto the forest floor, crunching pine needles underfoot. Rob followed. Calvin looked around him. He still didn't see anything. They walked across the forest floor.

"Well, here we go again," Calvin said, as they turned onto the trail. It led them over tree roots and rocks. Soon, the trail turned away from the creek. The sounds of the rushing water grew fainter. Every now and then, a smaller trail would branch off the main trail. But Calvin watched carefully for the trail signs. They weren't going to get lost, he told himself.

They had been walking quite a while when Calvin stopped and pointed at something.

"Look over there," Calvin cried.

Rob looked. Way off to the right of the trail were what looked like huge trees lying on their sides.

"Wow!" Rob exclaimed. "Those are giant!"

"How big are they? They must be six feet across," Calvin agreed.

"Let's go look at them!" Rob said.

The boys left the trail and jogged toward the enormous logs.

"They're farther away than I thought," Calvin said, panting.

"I know," Rob agreed, out of breath. "They looked like they were closer."

Finally, they reached the huge logs.

"What do you think happened to them, Mr. Wilderness Expert? What does it say in those adventure books you read?" Rob joked.

Calvin's face turned a little warm. He inspected the logs. He walked around one of the huge trees. "I don't know," he admitted. "Maybe they were struck by lightning. What do you think?"

Rob shrugged. "I dunno. Loggers, maybe?"

"Not in a national park, I don't think," Calvin said.

Rob grabbed onto one of the broken branches of the tree next to him. He hoisted himself onto a huge log. Then he ran down the length of the tree, jumping over small branches. "Hey! This is cool!" he said, grinning.

Calvin pulled himself up on the log next to Rob's.

"Race ya!" Calvin challenged.

"Yeah—but I got a bum ankle," Rob said.

"Excuses, always excuses, you wimp," Calvin said.

"Okay, fine," Rob said, a little angrily. "Ready? Set? Go!"

The boys took off. Their tennis shoes pounded on the logs. Calvin jumped over little branches. He dodged big ones. He could hear Rob's panting as he raced to the end of his log.

"Hah! Beat ya!" taunted Calvin. He wiped his forehead with his sleeve.

"Not by much," Rob said. "I'll get you next time," he said.

Calvin dropped down on the log. He was breathing hard. "Whew," he said. He noticed a huge knothole in the trunk. It was big enough for an animal. Well, a small one.

"Hey, Rob, look at this," he called. Rob looked over at Calvin's tree.

"Yeah?" he asked.

"Check this out," Calvin said. "I bet there's an animal in here. Let's see if we can get it to come out."

"Okay!" Rob said, grinning. He slid down the side of his tree. He pulled himself up onto Calvin's tree. Together, the boys peered into the dark hole.

"Don't stick your face down in there, you idiot," Calvin warned. "Some raccoon will bite your nose off."

"Or maybe a snake," Rob said.

"Where's a rock?" Calvin asked. "Let's throw a rock down there and see what happens. Maybe we can catch whatever it is and take it home. We'll be trappers!"

"It smells like an animal lives in there," Rob said, sniffing.

"Sick," Calvin said. He slid down off the tree. He hunted for some small rocks, and stuffed some into his pockets. Then he climbed back up.

"Ka-pow! Ka-pow!" Rob said. He fired two rocks into the hole.

"Did you hear anything?" Calvin asked.

"Not yet," Rob said. "Ka-pow! Ka-pow!" Two more rocks landed inside.

The boys leaned over and listened.

"Nah. I don't hear anything," Rob said. "Guess we weren't meant to be trappers." He grinned at Calvin.

"Guess we're just hikers," Calvin said. "Geez!" he exclaimed. He looked at his watch. "It's getting late. Let's get back to the trail."

They slid off the logs and began walking back toward the trail.

Calvin stopped suddenly. "Did we come this way?" He looked puzzled. "I don't remember these huge rocks here."

Rob stopped too. "I—I don't know. I was just watching the logs ahead. I guess I wasn't paying attention to where I was going."

"Great," Calvin said. "Now what?" He frowned. Think, Calvin, think, he told himself. He took a breath. "Okay. Let's face the logs so they look the way they did from the trail, okay? Then all we have to do is retrace our steps."

"All right," Rob agreed. They began to walk slowly in a circle, looking at the logs.

"Here!" Calvin said when they got to one side of the huge trees. "This is what they looked like, didn't they?"

"Yeah, I guess so," Rob said slowly.

"Well, all we can do is try it," Calvin said. "I think it's the right way," he said, trying to sound confident. The boys began walking slowly in a straight line, back toward where they hoped the trail was. Every now and then, they would turn around, making sure they kept the same view of the logs. Rob was quiet. He doesn't have any jokes now, Calvin thought.

7
The First Plunge

"All right!" Calvin hollered. There was the trail, clearly marked. The friendly green sign greeted them. He had never been so happy to see just plain dirt.

"Great!" Rob breathed. "I don't think I was ready to spend the night on this mountain. Too much weird stuff going on," he said.

Calvin looked at him curiously. "I thought you were the one who kept telling me everything was okay," he said. "That back in the cabin, it was just a homeless person, not an escaped prisoner. That what I saw at the boulders wasn't a mountain lion."

Rob looked sheepish. "Well, yeah," he said. "I always say stuff—so I don't get afraid," he admitted.

"Oh, good," Calvin said. "So you really *do* think that we could be in trouble up here?" He frowned.

"Well," Rob hedged. "Not really."

"But maybe?" Calvin asked.

"It could always be maybe," Rob said. "Anyway, I bet it's time to turn back. Look at the sun."

The boys squinted at the sun. Sure enough, Calvin thought in surprise. The sun was lower in the sky. What time was it, anyway? How much time had they wasted on the logs? How much time had it taken them to find the trail again? He looked at his watch and groaned.

"We'll never make it back before dark," Calvin said worriedly.

"Why not?" Rob asked.

"It's already three o'clock. The sun sets at six-thirty. But it starts getting dark earlier than that. And when we were at the boulders, we'd already been gone two hours. That was quite a ways back up the trail too." Calvin frowned. "And we don't have a flashlight now, either."

"That's okay," Rob joked. "Maybe we can stay the night with the escaped murderers in the abandoned cabin. We can catch the mountain lion and cook him for dinner." He grinned.

"Ha! Ha!" Calvin said crossly. "You're the comedian now, huh? Well, this isn't *Saturday Night Live*," he said. He hoped it wouldn't turn out to be *Saturday Night* Dead.

"Sorry. You know me," Rob admitted. He sighed and leaned against a tree trunk. "So, great hiking expert, what would your books say to do now?" he asked.

Calvin sat down on a rock. He frowned. He rested his chin in his hands. Then he looked up at Rob. "You know, I did read something sort of like this," he said slowly.

"Ah, come on! Do you expect me to believe that?" Rob asked. He shook his head.

"No, really," Calvin said. He stood up, brushing pine needles off his jeans. "These guys were lost. So they found a stream, and they followed it all the way down. Streams always run downhill, right?"

"Hey, yeah!" Rob said excitedly. He stopped leaning against the tree. He stood up straight. "And it's the same creek we saw at the entrance to the park, right? San Miguel Creek!" He grinned.

"Yeah! It would be a lot quicker to follow the creek down. I'm sure we're almost to the bottom of the mountain anyway. It makes sense to follow the creek. Otherwise, we'd have to go all the way back up the trail to the ranger station. Then we'd have to hike all the way back down the firebreak road! That's it! A shortcut!" Calvin almost shouted.

They were going to make it now. And they were going to have a real adventure! He grinned at Rob.

"So, where's the creek?" Rob asked. "We haven't seen it for a while."

Calvin stopped. "Yeah, that's right. That's kind of funny, actually. I don't know why the trail doesn't follow the stream the whole way," he said.

"Well, the rangers probably wanted to make it a longer hike or something," Rob suggested.

"Yeah. Following the stream all the time would probably be boring," Calvin added. "Anyway, I think we can find it. Listen," he said.

The boys strained their ears. Did they hear rushing water? Or was that the pine trees?

"I hear it! I hear it!" Rob yelled. He pointed off to the left. "Let's go."

"Let's be sure to keep the sun in the same direction," Calvin warned. He looked over his shoulder at the sun. It was dropping even lower in the sky. "We don't want to be going in circles, like the lost guys in books."

The two boys took off at a trot. Yes, Calvin thought excitedly. That was the stream! He could definitely hear it now. The sound of rushing water grew louder and louder. As they jogged around a grouping of huge boulders, they saw it.

"Yes!" Calvin shouted.

"All right!" Rob echoed. "Give me five!" He stuck his hand in the air.

"Okay, here we go," Calvin said. "We'll just stick by the side of the stream. We should be back down and home in no time."

Instead of flowing through open country, the stream was flowing through a canyon. The walls of the canyon were a lot steeper too, Calvin noticed. He looked downstream. It looked as if the canyon got narrower too. They would just have to stick closer to the stream. As long as they did that, they couldn't go wrong.

Calvin began to scramble over rocks. Rob followed.

"Uh-oh! Look out for this!" Calvin called after a few minutes. He stopped. Right where he stood, the rocks spilled down into the rushing water. Their side of the canyon wall began to close in on the stream.

Calvin looked downstream. There the steep rock wall plunged straight down into the frothing water. What could they do? There was no place to walk on this side. He felt a little twinge of fear. He looked at the other side of the stream. Whew. The other side looked good. Now all they had to do was get to the other side.

"We're gonna have to cross the stream," Calvin said when Rob caught up.

"Where do we cross?" Rob asked. They looked downstream.

"I don't see any rocks we can use as stepping stones,

do you?" Calvin asked.

"Nope," Rob answered slowly. Without a word, they turned and looked upstream.

"Not there either," Calvin said.

"Nope," Rob said.

Calvin tightened his mouth. Then he narrowed his eyes. "Okay," he said. "We'll have to swim or wade across."

"What?" Rob exclaimed. "You gotta be kidding! The creek's pretty wide. We don't know how deep it is either."

"No, I'm not kidding," Calvin said. "It couldn't be very deep. Besides, it's not *that* wide. You do laps, don't you?" he asked.

"Yeah," Rob said slowly. "But that's in a pool, where there's no current pulling me."

"Who's the wimp now?" Calvin asked.

Rob frowned. "Okay, fine. It looks like we don't have a choice anyway." He sighed. "It's gonna be awfully cold."

Calvin began taking off his shoes. "Tie your shoes to your belt loops," he said. "Be sure your jacket is tied tightly around your waist. We'll start walking through it. If we have to swim for it, at least we won't lose anything."

Rob took off his shoes too. "Good thing your watch is waterproof," he joked weakly.

"This *is* a real adventure," Calvin said with a grin. He took a deep breath and began wading into the rushing water.

"Whoa!" he yelled. His feet slipped on some smooth rocks under the water. Almost before he knew it, the current swept him off his feet.

Splash! Calvin fell into the rushing water.

8

Swim for It!

"Hey!" Calvin yelled. He splashed and struggled to his feet. The creek bed wasn't too deep. So the current had swept him just to his knees. Of course, now he was dripping wet. And the backpack was soaked too.

"Good thing this creek isn't that deep," he hollered to Rob, who was still standing on the other bank. He still looked frightened.

Calvin waded to the other side. He sat down on a big smooth rock to rest.

"I thought you were a goner," Rob said, recovering.

"Watch out for those slippery stones on the bottom. That's what happened to me," Calvin warned. He began squeezing water out of his clothes. He untied his shoes and held them upside down. Water streamed out.

"Great," he said. "Everything is wet."

Rob reached the other side. He joined Calvin and sat down to put his shoes on.

"At least you don't have to hike in wet shoes and socks," Calvin said. "Well," he sighed, standing up, "let's go."

They made their way down the canyon. Sometimes they hopped over rocks. Sometimes they had to climb over bigger ones. Next to them, the creek frothed and bubbled around rocks. Sometimes there was even some white water where the creek surged over rocks in the middle.

"Whew," Rob said. "My ankle's bugging me. Let's rest for a while. We've been going for about half an hour, don't you think?"

"Sure," Calvin agreed. "All the rest of our food is soaked." He made a face as he opened the backpack. "But we can still drink the soda," he said. He handed a can to Rob.

Calvin tipped the can up to drink. Something caught his eye. Something above them flashed—he knew it.

"Hey!" he said, setting the can down suddenly. He stared at the opposite canyon wall. "Did you see something up there?" he whispered to Rob. His heart raced. Stop, he told himself. Don't be so jumpy.

"Uh, I—I'm not sure," Rob said slowly. He looked up again where Calvin pointed. "Uh—no—no, I don't think so," he said. Then he stared down at his shoes. He rubbed his soda can between his palms, back and forth.

What was going on with Rob? Calvin wondered. He wasn't acting like himself.

"What's up with you, man?" Calvin demanded. "Are you going psycho on me or something?"

Rob didn't answer Calvin. He stared at his feet.

Rob did look kind of green, Calvin thought. What was wrong with him?

Rob took a breath. "I think I've been seeing stuff," he admitted.

"What?!" Calvin blurted out. His stomach turned a flip. "What do you mean you've been seeing stuff? Why didn't you tell me?!"

"Well, a while ago, I thought I saw something moving up above us on the cliff," Rob said slowly. He seemed to be forcing his words out. "But every time I looked for it again, it was gone.

"Then I thought I heard something rustling in the bushes on our side of the stream," he continued. "But I thought it was just the wind or a bird. Or maybe the creek was extra loud."

Rob stopped. He looked at Calvin. "I didn't tell you because I wasn't sure myself. I didn't want to get you worried. I know you're already thinking about those prisoners. And then you thought you saw a mountain lion back there by the boulders," Rob finished.

Calvin sighed disgustedly. "So you were trying to protect me?" he asked angrily. "I don't need protection. Just talk to me straight. Things will be fine then."

"Sorry, okay?" Rob said. He looked miserable.

"Yeah, no problem. Forget it," Calvin said.

"But now you see it too. What do we do?" Rob asked.

Calvin looked around. The steep canyon walls were closing in on them. Even the side they were on was losing ground to the sheer rock walls. He studied the canyon walls. They were steep. It would be impossible to climb them in a hurry. Every now and then, a ledge jutted out from the canyon wall. Lone trees and a few bushes grew bravely from the loose rock walls, reaching up to the sunlight. But there was no easy escape if something—or someone—were to come after them.

"Well," Calvin said. "It looks like we're not going anywhere but down. We just have to keep going. And hope. Maybe it's just a deer. Maybe it's a raccoon or something. Whatever it is, we have to forget it. Let's concentrate on just gettin' out of here."

The other side of the stream was already in a shadow, Calvin noticed. They really did have to keep moving.

"Okay. My ankle's okay," Rob said. "Let's move." He got up and pulled Calvin to his feet.

They both shot a quick glance to the top of the opposite cliff. Calvin wondered what was up there. Just forget it, he told himself. He had enough to worry about. He didn't need to imagine things too.

They rounded the next bend.

"Oh, no!" Calvin yelled.

The canyon walls on both sides had closed in. The creek rushed forward into a waterfall. It plunged about four feet down into a pool and then re-formed into the creek again. Then the creek bank widened out a little on their side. But right here, there was no place for them to go. They were trapped.

"What now?" Rob asked.

"We've gotta jump down the waterfall," Calvin said.

"What?" Rob squawked. "With my ankle?"

"We don't have a choice," Calvin said. "We don't have the time to go back before it gets dark. There's no place to climb up out of the canyon. We have to jump it."

Calvin walked closer to the edge of the rocks. He looked down the waterfall. "Look," he said. "It's not that far. We can jump and land on our feet. We don't have to worry about hitting our heads on any rocks or anything," he added.

"But we don't know how deep it is," Rob said.

"I bet it's not very deep," Calvin said. "Besides, so what if it is? You can just swim up to the top. This is just a mountain stream, not the high dive, you know."

Rob sighed. "All right," he said. He knelt next to Calvin. Calvin was already taking off his shoes.

Calvin teetered on the edge. Rob watched him.

Calvin bent his knees. He held his breath.

"Yahoo!" he hollered. Then he jumped into the pool. He bounced back up through the foaming water. The water was only to his waist.

"Come on, you chicken!" he called to Rob. "Bawk-bawk-bawk!" he cried, flapping his arms.

Rob held his breath and jumped.

"Aah!" he yelled, coming back up in a spray of water. "That didn't feel too good on my ankle," he said.

"Come on, let's get over to the bank," Calvin said. The boys waded slowly through the water. They climbed onto the bank. Water ran in streams from their jeans and their shoes. They took a few moments to untie their shoes and empty the water out.

"Sick," Rob said. "It feels like I have sea slugs inside my shoes."

"Yeah, well that's what mine have felt like for the last half hour," Calvin reminded him. "Get up. We gotta go."

In the next few minutes, they came to a second small waterfall. Calvin and Rob groaned. They sat down and went through the routine. Tie shoes onto belts. Jump in. Wade back to shore.

Then, around the next bend, another waterfall plunged down into a pool.

"This is gettin' old, man," Calvin complained.

"No kidding," Rob agreed.

"At least we're getting down off the mountain," Calvin said. The shadows had lengthened. They were no longer in sunlight. The cliffs cast dark shadows through the canyon.

They finished their usual routine and trudged on.

"Boy, the creek is sure getting louder," Rob said.

"Yeah, we must be getting down to the bottom," Calvin guessed.

"That would be great," Rob said with a smile.

They rounded the next bend.

Calvin saw it first. Then his heart sank to his shoes. This is bad, he thought. This is *really* bad.

9

Trapped

"Geez," Calvin breathed. The roar of the waterfall echoed against the canyon walls. The mountain sides seemed to force the creek into a narrow chute. It roared between jagged rocks. Then it plunged straight down into a dark pool at the bottom. Huge rocks lined the pool below.

"How high a waterfall do you think it is?" Rob asked worriedly.

Calvin measured it with his eyes. "It must be 12 or 15 feet," he said. His shoulders slumped. "Geez," he repeated.

"Do we jump into this one too?" Rob asked. He twisted the cuffs of his jacket around and around.

"I don't think so," Calvin said slowly.

"We did the others," Rob said. "Maybe we could do this one."

"Look at it," Calvin said. "Be serious. This is way too high. And we have no idea what's at the bottom of the pool. Or where the bottom is. Check out those rocks at the side. There could be more of them under the water."

Calvin turned to look at Rob. "Don't you remember that video we saw in health class? The one about diving and getting paralyzed? I don't feel like ending up in a wheelchair."

"So," Rob said, "what are our choices? Hope for a rescue? Wait for the mountain lion to attack after the sun goes down? Or should we just wait for the escaped prisoners to jump us in the dark?" Rob swallowed hard. He lowered his voice. "You know—we *both* know—something is stalking us." He looked quickly around them.

Rob really looks scared, Calvin thought. It was about time he took this hike seriously.

"Well, we could think about working our way back up the creek," Calvin said. "Then we could find the trail. When it gets too dark to see, we could spend the night under some fallen branches or something. Then in the morning, we could get back to the ranger station."

"Great. Yeah, we could do that. That is, if there isn't anything—or anyone—out there after us," Rob grumbled. "Besides, our clothes are wet. We'll freeze up here at night."

"We can build a fire," Calvin offered. "Mountain lions won't come near a fire," he said. "We'll take turns staying awake. That way, we can watch it all night. Then it won't start a forest fire."

"Ready to actually break the rules?" Rob joked.

"Well," Calvin stopped, "this is survival."

"Where are the matches?" Rob asked.

"Right in the—" Calvin's face fell. He hurriedly unslung the backpack. He unzipped it. His hands rummaged through it. Then he held up a dripping matchbook.

"This isn't so much fun anymore," Rob said slowly. "I'm not enjoying this adventure. And you know what?" he continued.

"What?" Calvin asked.

"I just thought of something. You know all those waterfalls we jumped down?" Rob stopped. He took a deep breath. "We can't jump *up* a waterfall." He looked like he could cry. "There's no way to climb up those waterfalls. We can't go back to the trail. We're trapped."

Calvin's blood ran cold. Rob was right. He knew it. He remembered all the waterfalls they had jumped down. They had been laughing and splashing. It had been a big adventure. They had felt like hot-shot outdoorsmen. And all that time, they had been sealing their own doom. There was no going back.

"Okay," Calvin said. His forehead was pounding. "Let's think about this for a minute." He looked around for something to sit on. He found a rock and sat down. Rob dropped down next to him with a sigh.

"Hiking. What a great idea," Rob grumbled. "I'm too young to die up here on a mountain."

In the half-light of the setting sun, Calvin studied the walls of the canyon. His eyes moved carefully over each slope. There. Right there. Maybe they could climb back up the canyon wall.

"Look," Calvin said. He pointed to the canyon wall just to the left of them. "See how it isn't so steep there? Halfway up, there's a ledge too. It sticks out enough to rest on. Then there's that tree up on top?"

"Uh-huh," Rob said. He strained his eyes to see in the gathering darkness.

"See how the roots are growing out of the rock wall. We could grab onto them and pull ourselves up."

"Well," Rob said, "I'll try anything to get out of here. But what do we do once we're up there?" he asked. "We'll still be lost."

"Not really," Calvin assured him. His voice became more excited as he thought about it. "We'll just follow the ridge of the canyon all the way along the creek. We'll be able to hear the creek below us. And remember, the trail meets the creek up there."

Trapped

"Yeah," Rob agreed. "Let's hope no mountain lion decides it's hungry."

"It's no use worrying about something we can't do anything about," Calvin said. He frowned. "Right now, we'd better move. We don't have long before it's dark."

"Okay," Rob said. He bent over and rubbed his ankle. Then he stretched and stood up. "Well, we've gotta do this."

"I'll go first," Calvin said. "That way, I can test what's loose. With your ankle, you have to be careful. You can't put much weight on it, right?"

Rob nodded. "My basketball coach is gonna be pretty ticked off at me for wrecking my ankle. *If* I ever see him again, that is," he grinned weakly.

Calvin began climbing the steep wall of the canyon. He found places in the rock to rest his feet. He reached up and found rocks that he could hold onto. Painfully, slowly, he worked his way up the cliff. He saw the ledge looming above him. Halfway! He reached up a hand. Please let it be solid rock, he prayed. If it was loose gravel and sand, they were in big trouble. His fingers spread out. There! It held! He reached out his other hand. That rock held too! He bounced a little on the balls of his feet. Then, muscles straining, he pulled himself onto the ledge.

"Way to go!" Rob's voice echoed against the canyon walls. "You did it!"

"Come on, man," Calvin encouraged. "It's not bad."

71

Rob began his slow climb up the side.

Calvin rested and watched for a moment. Then he stood up. He took a deep breath and began to finish his climb.

Slowly, slowly, Calvin inched his way up the canyon wall. Ahead were the tree roots! He reached up and grabbed on with one hand. Then he shifted his weight. He reached out the other hand. Got it! He began to pull himself up over the top.

Suddenly, the ground gave way under him. He began to slip.

"Aaah!" he yelled. Loose rocks and gravel rattled down the sides of the cliff. He grabbed tightly to the tree roots. He powered all his strength into one pull.

"Unnh!" he groaned. He made it! He was on top! He lay there for a moment, panting. Then he scrambled to his feet.

"I made it, Rob!" he yelled. "Be careful, though. It's slippery on top!"

Calvin peered over the side. The shadows were deepening in the canyon. He could see Rob's face and white jacket moving up the canyon wall toward him. He had made it past the ledge. Now he was almost to the tree roots.

"Okay, Rob," Calvin encouraged. "You almost got it. Here—grab my hand."

Calvin reached out his hand to help pull Rob up. Just then he began to slide. "No!" he yelled.

10
The Light in the Cabin

"No!" Calvin yelled again. Desperately, with his free arm, he grabbed onto the tree trunk. His sliding stopped. Safe! His heart pounded. That was too close. He could hear rocks and gravel sliding and bouncing down the canyon sides.

"Ouch! Dang!" Rob hollered. "All these rocks! What're you doin', man?"

"Shut up," Calvin said. "Just grab my hand, will you?" He just hoped the tree would hold. It should. It felt sturdy enough.

"Unnh!" Rob groaned. Rob's sweaty hand grabbed Calvin's.

"Now just grab a tree root, and I'll help pull you up," Calvin said. "Just bounce yourself up. You know, like you're going for a rebound."

"Aaaah! My ankle!" Rob moaned. But Calvin yanked at the same time.

Thud! He pulled Rob up over the side. A shower of gravel and loose rocks tumbled down the canyon.

"Thanks, man," Rob panted.

"Let's get away from this edge," Calvin gasped. He was out of breath too.

Calvin stood up and brushed off his jeans. "Now all we should have to do is follow the ridgeline back," he said.

"Yeah. So long as we don't meet up with any mountain lion or escaped prisoner," Rob croaked hoarsely. He limped behind Calvin.

"Stay close, man," Calvin warned.

"I'm trying. I'm trying," Rob said.

Moving quickly, they hiked along the top of the cliff. Calvin could hear the creek roaring below. All those little waterfalls made a lot of noise when they echoed. They must have been crazy to try that.

"No wonder the trail didn't follow the stream all the

way down," Calvin said after they'd been hiking a while.

"Yeah, you're right," Rob said gloomily. "Guess the rangers knew more than we did. Ow!" he yelped. He stopped.

"What happened?" Calvin asked as he turned to wait for Rob.

"Aw, I just tripped over something. A tree root or a rock. I dunno. It's hard to see where I'm going," Rob complained. "It's getting dark."

"Uh-huh," Calvin agreed. It was getting dark. Pretty soon, it would be too dark to hike. Even now it was scary. Calvin was afraid they might get too close to the edge of the cliff in the dark. He shuddered. It would be a long way to fall.

"Aaaaah!" Calvin croaked in a hoarse whisper. He reached a hand back to stop Rob.

"What is it?" Rob asked.

Calvin was paralyzed with fear. He held Rob's arm in a death grip. He was sure his heart would explode right out of his chest.

"Look!" Calvin whispered. "Over there through the trees. Two people—sitting on a log."

"It's the escapees!" Rob whispered. "Oh my gosh. We're gonna die!"

Calvin squinted his eyes and looked. "No," he whispered back. "No, I don't think so." He peered through the gloom. "Uh-uh," he said. "Not unless one of the guys is a girl."

"Who then?" Rob demanded.

"It's—I think it's—yup!" Calvin whispered. "It's some homeless people. It's a woman and a man. Looks like they have a bundle of stuff with them."

"Let's get the heck out of here," Rob urged.

"Okay," Calvin agreed. "They don't want us to see them anyway. Let's just keep walking. We'll pretend we didn't see them. They probably don't want to be found. Just like Harold said."

They continued through the forest, trying to walk quietly. Every now and then, a twig crunched under their shoes.

Rob suddenly stiffened. "Did you hear that?" he whispered.

Calvin froze. In the underbrush. He heard it too. Something was rustling and moving around.

"Oh, geez," he said. "Let's get moving. I think I read that if you yell and sing, some animals will be afraid. They'll go away. But if you're afraid—" he stopped for a moment. He swallowed hard. "If you're afraid, the animals can smell it on you. Then they attack."

"Great," Rob said. "So just don't be afraid. Is that the answer?" he joked weakly. "Okay. I'm not afraid. Ha-ha, mountain lion!"

"That's not too far wrong," Calvin said. "Let's get moving. And let's sing some songs or something."

"Sing?!" Rob exclaimed. "Like what? What songs do we both know that we can sing?"

"How about—how about Christmas carols? 'The Star-Spangled Banner'? 'A Thousand Bottles of—' "

"Okay, okay. I get the picture." Rob cleared his throat. "Oh, say can you see—"

"By the dawn's early light—" Calvin's voice joined Rob's as they hurried along the ridge.

They were just finishing "The First Noel" when Calvin saw something glimmering in the distance. "Look!" he cried. He pulled Rob to a stop. "It's a light! I think we're close to the cabins!"

"How could we be?" Rob asked. "We haven't even found the trail yet. The cabins were a ways down the trail, weren't they?"

"Yeah, they were. But the trail didn't go in a straight line, stupid. It followed the creek for a long time. Do creeks run straight? No, they don't," Calvin said disgustedly. "So the trail probably wound around and around. The cabins are probably in a straight line from here. That's why we can see the light."

"Wait a second," Rob said. "Why are we seeing a light?" He stopped. "Weren't those cabins empty?" he asked slowly.

"Look at the light too," Calvin said hoarsely. They watched in silence. "It's moving around, isn't it?"

"Who's in the cabins?" Rob asked softly. "Who could it be?"

Calvin's stomach flipped. "Well, somebody is," he said. "Unless somebody has a light on a timer. Which doesn't make sense for a cabin in the forest. And a light on a timer wouldn't move around," he admitted. "It could be some more homeless people. Or—I—ah—don't really want to say this. But," he said, taking a deep breath, "it could be those escaped prisoners." Calvin stopped. His heart pounded. "Hey—if it is, I bet they scared the home-less people out of the cabin!"

"That's what I was thinking," Rob said. He looked worried. "How would the prisoners get a light, though?"

Calvin and Rob looked at each other in horror.

"Our flashlight!" they said together.

"We'll have to sneak by the cabins," Calvin said. "We can't let them find us."

"Why do we even have to go near the cabins?" Rob asked.

"That's where the trail is, lamebrain," Calvin said. "We won't get that close, though. We'll just have to be sure we don't lose the trail."

Rob looked up at the sky through the trees. Its purple shade was deepening. Faint orange rinsed the sky in the west. The sun was finally down.

"Well, I hope it's a full moon anyway," Rob whis-pered. "Then we'll have a chance of seeing the trail."

"No more singing, now," Calvin whispered back. "I'd rather take my chances with a mountain lion than with some criminals."

Why can't we walk more quietly? Calvin wondered. He tried putting his foot down toe first. Maybe that would do it. But every step he took through the pine needles seemed to crackle like gunfire.

"We're so noisy," Rob whispered.

"I know," Calvin answered back in a low voice.

They moved on. The light grew brighter. It flickered for a while. Then it held steady. They stole closer and closer to the group of cabins.

Calvin's hands were clammy. He remembered being afraid before some football games. But he had never been this afraid before!

Calvin crouched low behind a huge rock. Rob joined him. Calvin peered around the rock. The group of cabins was about a hundred yards away.

"We have to make it across this clearing," he whispered. "Then we'll run for the trail. It's a short way from there to the ranger's station. Can you make it with your ankle?"

"I've got to," Rob replied.

Just then, the boys heard a cabin door open. Someone walked slowly across a porch. Calvin hardly dared breathe.

Then—a car door opened and shut. Wait, Calvin thought. A car door? He squinted his eyes, trying to see.

Headlights pierced the darkness. Slowly, a truck began moving through the clearing. On the door was painted "U.S. Forest Service."

Calvin jumped up. "Yes! Yes!" he yelled. "We're saved!" He rushed into the clearing, waving his arms.

Rob followed, yelling.

"Hey! Hey!" they cried.

The truck stopped and it backed up. The side window rolled down just as Calvin and Rob reached the truck.

A frowning face looked out at them from under a ranger's hat. "Are you two Calvin and Rob?" the ranger asked.

"Yeah! Yeah, we are! You found us!" Calvin said excitedly.

"You two are pretty foolish kids," the ranger said as she shook her head. "We've been looking all over for you. We've had a couple of reports of mountain lion sightings today from hikers. Get in. Your families are worried sick about you."

Gratefully, Calvin and Rob climbed into the front seat next to the ranger. Rob slammed the door. Calvin leaned back against the seat in relief. He and Rob grinned at each other.

They had made it! Calvin thought. They had made it out of the canyon!

"So," Rob turned to him, still grinning. "When are we going hiking again, Great Wilderness Expert?"

Calvin almost choked. The ranger turned to look at him.

"Ah—any time you want to!" Calvin said.